How Did You Come to School Today?

Gail Fleming

How Did You Come to School Today?

Gail Fleming

AuthorReputationPress®
Creativity & Branding

How did you come
To school today?

Was it in a balloon?
UP..UP..and AWAY!!

Or did you just float
in on a boat?

Did you ride in a truck?

Waddle in on a duck?

9

Did you fly in a plane?

Or take a small train?

Perhaps, of course,
You came on a horse!

Like Great Grandma did
When she was a kid!

A bike is for ME,
On two wheels or three.

19

By van, car or train,
You are here just the same

21

So let's give a cheer!
I'm so glad you're here.

To Daniel, who came in a van.

Author Reputation Press LLC
45 Dan Road Suite 5
Canton MA 02021
www.authorreputationpress.com
Hotline: 1(888) 821-0229
Fax: 1(508) 545-7580

Ordering Information:
Quantity sales. Special discounts are available on quantity purchases by corporations, associations, and others. For details, contact the publisher at the address above.

Printed in the United States of America.

ISBN-13:   Softcover   979-8-88853-874-6
           Hardcover   979-8-88853-877-7
           eBook   979-8-88853-875-3

Library of Congress Control Number: 2023917989

Milton Keynes UK
Ingram Content Group UK Ltd.
UKHW051138301123
433523UK00002B/47